DK Publishing, Inc.
95 Madison Avenue
New York, New York 10016

Visit us on the World Wide Web at http://www.dk.com

ISBN 0-7894-3490-3

The text for this book is set in 24 point Weiss.

Published simultaneously in the United Kingdom
by Dorling Kindersley Ltd., 9 Henrietta Street, London, WC2E 8PS

Printed and bound in Singapore by Tien Wah Press

First American Edition, 1998
2 4 6 8 10 9 7 5 3 1

For Chris and Julian – S.G.
For Grandma – J.C.

A Flag for Grandma

Sally Grindley

Illustrated by Jason Cockcroft

A DK INK BOOK
DK PUBLISHING, INC.

GRANDPA LIVES IN a house by the sea.

"What, you again?" he says

when I go there to stay.

"Me again," I laugh,

and we wrestle like schoolboys.

He's still the same old Grandpa,

can't wait for the next day.

WE'RE UP WHEN the gulls stir,
the sea mist just clearing,
hot breakfast, cold picnic packed,
fishing nets waiting.

THEN WE'RE OFF down the cliff path,

all winding and bumpy,

all pebbly and sliding,

Grandpa in front,

whistling tunes through his whiskers,

and me just behind,

blowing air through dry lips.

The beach is our playground.

The sand traps our footprints,

tells tales of our races;

"Can't catch me," says Grandpa.

I can, but I won't.

The sand frames our pictures
for Grandma, "We miss you,"
till the sea turns spoilsport
and drags them away.

W E BUILD OUR sandcastles

with turrets and peepholes.

"This flag is for Grandma."

I place it with care.

A driftwood portcullis

stands guard at the entrance,

a forest of seaweed

circles the keep.

WE PICNIC ON the jetty,
hurl crumbs for the seagulls.
Grandpa steals sleep,
drifting off with the waves.

I peer through the water,

small fishes flash silver.

My coin carries wishes

for Grandpa and me.

WE SCAMPER UP sand dunes,
clamber round tide pools,
our fishing nets billow
round hide-and-seek crabs.
"Not more," Grandpa groans
when I dig out a fossil;
our pockets weigh heavy.
"Just one," I grin back.

WE STAND ON the water's edge,
trousers rolled knee-high,
"This big leap's for Grandma,"
shouts Grandpa midair.

I catch hold of his arm

and we jump the foam rivers

till our toes get all wrinkly

and our feet are sand sore.

THEN IT'S BACK up the cliff path,

all winding and bumpy,

all pebbly and sliding,

Grandpa in front, wheezing,

"Too old," through his whiskers,

and me just behind,

breathing in the salt air.

WE STAND AND look out
where the moonlight is shining.
A silver road stretches
from ocean to sky.

"That's the path Grandma took,"
whispers Grandpa, eyes sparkling.
I hold his hand tight
as the path fades to cloud.

GRANDPA'S HOUSE COMFORTS us,

cozy chairs, warm fire,

hot soup, thick bread,

and we're yawning for bed.

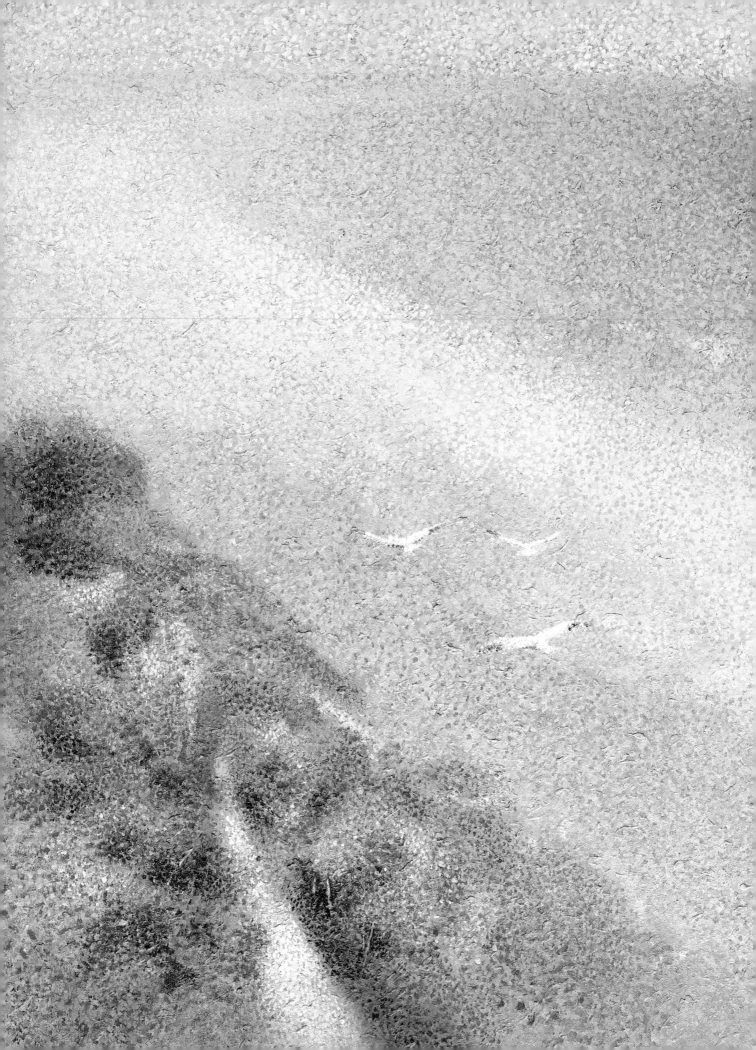

We'll be up when the gulls stir,

the sea mist just clearing,

then off down the cliff path,

just Grandpa and me.